The TALE of SIR DRAGON

Dealing with Bullies for Kids
(and DRAGONS)

Written by Jean E. Pendziwol
Illustrated by Martine Gourbault

To the trustworthy
and noble Jamshid.

Jan 14

Kids Can Press

One hot August day at the end of last week,
I went to meet Dragon, who lives near the creek.

He carried a shield and his teddy did, too,
So I cheered, "Come on, Dragon, I know what we'll do!"

We were going together to camp for the day,
But first we had to get ready to play.

Hand in hand we raced home and I grabbed what I could:
Scissors, glue, cardboard, tape, tinfoil and wood.

We snipped and we cut, we glued, then at last
We both donned the armor of ages long past.

Raising my sword, I cried, "From east to west!
From north to south on a knight's noble quest!"

"To the park!" Dad joined in. "Set off at a trot!
It's time to head out to Camp Camelot."

When we got to the drawbridge, Dad hugged us good-bye.
We went off to play, the dragon and I.

Through the playground we jousted, a chivalrous pair,
Till we bumped into three other knights standing there.

One of them sneered, "Well, what have we here?"
And I looked at the dragon, whose eyes filled with fear.

"A dragon!" He smirked. "We've told you before,
You're too big, tall and green to play knights anymore!

"Let's chase him away!" he cried, raising his shield.
"We'll vanquish that dragon! We'll make that beast yield!"

My poor friend the dragon, his head hanging low,
Turned around sadly and started to go.

But that bully wasn't done. With a blistering stare,
He boldly walked up and snatched Dragon's bear!

"Wait a minute!" I cried. "What you're doing's not right;
The dragon's a trustworthy, most valiant knight!

"No one should ever be treated this way;
Give back his bear and let's all of us play."

Surprised at my outburst, he laughed, "Can't be done!
Dragons aren't knights and they can't join the fun."

With that, all three left. I stood there and frowned.
A fat dragon teardrop fell to the ground.

"I know what to do. I know just the thing."
I smiled. "Let's petition for help from the King."

It took but a moment to reach the King's court,
And bowing quite humbly, I gave my report.

"A serious charge," he said, "I must agree.
I'm glad that you both brought this issue to me.

"I'll send a command and as quick as they're able,
We'll meet with them here around the round table."

My good friend the dragon, big, tall and green,
Went off for a walk hand in hand with the Queen.

As soon as the group of knights could be found,
The bully, his friends and I gathered around.

The King asked us, "What does it mean to belong?
Was treating the dragon that way right or wrong?"

"Have you ever felt picked on?" I asked. "Have you felt small?
Have you felt like there's no one who likes you at all?"

We sat there awhile, no one making a sound,
And then the mean knight said, looking around,

"It doesn't feel good, I have to admit.
I've been picked on before; I don't like it one bit.

"I've been told I'm too little and too young to play,
But I didn't think dragons would feel left out that way."

The King said to the boy, "I'll make this quite clear:
We'll have absolutely no bullying here.

"Go on a quest to fix what you've done wrong,
And think about how you can all get along."

Bowing low to the King, as all proper knights do,
He agreed to the quest and we all then withdrew.

Excalibur

It wasn't much later, as we sat eating lunch,
That Dragon and I again saw that bunch.

My friend sat up tall, his head held up high,
And he looked at the bully, right in the eye.

"You can play," the knight said. "What I did wasn't fair."
Then he reached out and gave back my friend's teddy bear.

On a scroll, together, we wrote a decree
That all knights, including the dragon and me,

Wouldn't take things or hurt or say anything mean.
Then we knelt and were honored by both King and Queen.

We Camelot knights of the King's round table
Each chose a horse from the playground stable,

And set off together, a bright merry band.
In search of adventure, we traveled the land.

By and by we heard faintly a cry of distress.
"To the rescue!" we hollered with brave nobleness.

We gathered, all five, at the base of a tree
Where a kitten was clinging precariously.

"It's no use, we can't reach," I said with a sigh.
"She's stuck in the branches, up way too high."

But Sir Dragon stepped forward and, stretching quite tall,
Grasped that poor kitten before she could fall!

He placed her quite gently back on the ground,
And cheering, we other knights crowded around.

"Hip, hip, hurray for the big, tall, green knight,
Who rescued the damsel from perilous plight!"

So we rode through the country performing great deeds,
Five noble knights on our trustworthy steeds.

And my good friend the dragon, who stood proud and tall,
Was the bravest and noblest knight of them all.

The Dragon's Decree

I will use my words and actions to help, not harm.

If ever I or someone else is bullied, I will get help.

I will not encourage a bully.

I will learn to accept others for who they are and treat them with kindness.

The dragon knows what it's like to be bullied and, with his friend, has taken steps to get help and resolve the situation. As you read *The Tale of Sir Dragon*, talk about what is happening to the dragon and child and what it means to be a bully, a victim and a bystander. It's important to discuss appropriate behavior with the children in your care, and what to do if they or others are being bullied. Emphasize being a positive bystander by getting help for the victim and not going along with the bullying by laughing or encouraging the bully's actions.

Remind your child that bullying isn't only when someone is picked on or hurt. Bullying is also not letting someone play or be part of a group, making fun of and laughing at someone, saying mean things to or about someone, threatening someone or taking something away from someone.

As parents, caregivers and educators, our most important role in breaking the bullying cycle is to help children learn empathy by looking for opportunities to teach kindness, tolerance and acceptance.

If you are being bullied, remember the following:

- It's not your fault! No one deserves to be bullied, and there's nothing wrong with you.

- Stand tall, try not to look scared, hold your head up high and walk away.

- Get help! It may be the hardest thing you do, but tell a parent, teacher or coach, and keep telling until someone listens and does something to help you.

- Don't bully the bully. Fighting back could cause more problems and is not a solution to bullying.

- Come up with a plan that will keep you safe until the problem is resolved. For example, you may want to take a different way home from school.

- Get involved with something that makes you feel good about yourself. Everybody is good at something!

Everyone can help stop bullying! Here is a checklist to discuss and put into action together:

- Remember to treat everyone the way you would like to be treated. Bullies often target people who are different in some way, such as how they look or dress. Learn to accept people for who they are. It is our differences that make each of us unique and special!

- Know the difference between tattling and telling. Tattling is done to get others in trouble. Telling is done to get help and to solve a problem.

- Tell an adult you trust if you or someone you know is being bullied. Keep telling until you get help.

- Be a positive bystander. Don't go along with bullying by laughing and cheering, or by agreeing with or encouraging the bully's behavior. Stand up for the victim. Tell the bully to stop, and tell an adult what is happening.

- Some bullies behave badly because they have problems of their own, and some are even bullied themselves. These are not excuses for their behavior, but may help the victim understand that the bully needs help, too.

- Find out if your school has an anti-bullying program. If not, help get one started. The program should include education about bullying, increased supervision and the setting and enforcing of rules and consequences.

For Sir Ryan the Noble, with love — J.E.P.

For Jennifer, my friend and inspiration — M.G.

Text © 2007 Jean E. Pendziwol
Illustrations © 2007 Martine Gourbault

With thanks to Tara Gauld, Health Promotion Planner, Early Child Development Injury and Family Abuse Prevention Program, Thunder Bay District Health Unit, and Constable Sean Mulligan, McKellar Neighbourhood Policing, City of Thunder Bay Police.

Kids Can Press acknowledges the financial support of the Government of Ontario, through the Ontario Media Development Corporation's Ontario Book Initiative; the Ontario Arts Council; the Canada Council for the Arts; and the Government of Canada, through the CBF, for our publishing activity.

Published in Canada by
Kids Can Press Ltd.
25 Dockside Drive
Toronto, ON M5A 0B5

Published in the U.S. by
Kids Can Press Ltd.
2250 Military Road
Tonawanda, NY 14150

www.kidscanpress.com

The artwork in this book was rendered in pencil crayon.
The text is set in Berkeley.

Edited by Debbie Rogosin
Designed by Karen Powers

The hardcover edition of this book is smyth sewn casebound.
The paperback edition of this book is limp sewn with a drawn-on cover.

Manufactured in Shenzen, China, in 11/2012 by C&C Offset Printing Co.

CM 07 0 9 8 7 6 5 4 3 2
CM PA 07 0 9 8 7 6 5 4 3

Library and Archives Canada Cataloguing in Publication

Pendziwol, Jean E.
   The tale of Sir Dragon : dealing with bullies for kids (and dragons) / written by Jean E. Pendziwol ; illustrated by Martine Gourbault.

For ages 3–7.

ISBN 978-1-55453-135-6 (bound)
ISBN 978-1-55453-136-3 (pbk.)

1. Bullying — Juvenile literature. I. Gourbault, Martine II. Title.

PS8581.E55312T35 2007   jC813'.54   C2006-903702-7

Kids Can Press is a *corus*™ Entertainment company